AF338243

Powered by Alexis Marie Productions Inc.

For permission, please address Wild Skies Press.

Published 2026
Printed in Canada

ISBN Paperback: 978-1-997770-11-4
ISBN E-Book: 978-1-997770-12-1

Cover Design by Alexis Marie Chute
Interior Design by Alexis Marie Chute
Stock media: Marylyn Gomez, Davyd Kopych, photosynthesis, Carkhe, joebelanger, rraya, Hase-Hoch-2, sudok1, masterSergeant, and nidwlw

For information or bulk orders address:
Wild Skies Press
A division of Alexis Marie Productions Inc.
Edmonton, Alberta, Canada
info@alexismariechute.com
www.WildSkiesPress.com

Wild Skies Press is an independent literary publisher founded in 2021. Wild Skies refers to the Aurora Borealis—northern lights—in Alberta, where the press is located, situated on Treaty 6 Territory. Wild Skies Press publishes non-fiction, fiction, poetry, and hybrid genres with an emphasis on the creation of books by emerging and established authors.

www.WildSkiesPress.com

*For my friends who read my drafts
over and over again.*

I hope you like this one.

A Queer Tale

Penguins Fly

Poems

Teren Hazzard

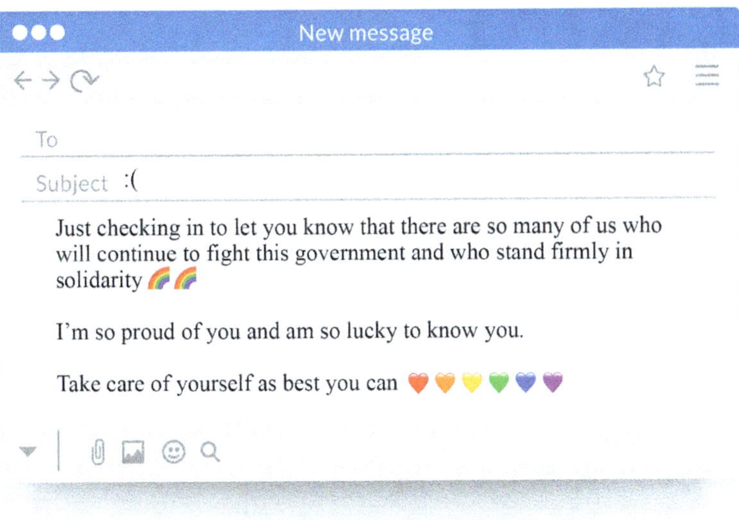

New message

To

Subject :(

Just checking in to let you know that there are so many of us who will continue to fight this government and who stand firmly in solidarity 🌈🌈

I'm so proud of you and am so lucky to know you.

Take care of yourself as best you can ❤️🧡💛💚💙💜

Poems

I am the keeper of the toys and pamphlets.
I am the stocker of the shelves. I am
the aquarium gift shop keyholder.
And this is only the first step to
becoming a penguin-ologist.
Flightless ornithologist? Antarctic
seagull scientist. I'll get there one day.
But first I must make friends with the
stuffed penguins and shark keychains,
my new coworkers until I move up
to blending fish guts, to cleaning penguin poo,
and to learning about these creatures
I cannot stop reading about, looking at.
After I help this next customer. Hello, miss!

I Think I Might Be Fired

"I steal marine animals while the
aquarium workers aren't looking" reads
her shirt. She basically wore a ski mask
to a bank robbery. We all see she is the
super villain of our dear aquarium. And
I see why she would want to steal these fluffballs.
I have certainly thought of it myself,
But… I still sneak by, and save the penguins
before she can get to them. See. I have
the keys 'cause I work at the gift shop
and she does not. She works at the Tim Hortons
where I buy my Iced Capps. She sneaks me
free donuts. She… turns and smiles at me.
And I… leave the enclosure unlocked.

SUGAR RUSH

Third coffee today.
Third attempt to say hello.
Caffeine, make me brave.

LesbianGoddess

Y'all I'm gonna ask her out.
I'mgoingtodoit. I'mgoingtodoit.
I'mgoingtodoit. I'mgoingtodoit.
I swear. I- OOF! I trip over my feet.
"Oh my god. Are you okay? I
saw you fall." Hands that smell of
sunscreen pull me to my feet.
"Hi. Yes. Yes. I'm fine. I'm-"
I meet her eyes. I choke on my
words. She grins. "You're QueerNameHere,
right? I see you at the kiosk all the time.
I love your skirts! I'm LesbianGoddess."

I give her flowers for our first, second, and third date.
She picks me up at the door in a sun dress, although
it is January. We go to the botanical gardens and I
bring a picnic basket, sandwiches, and a checkered blanket.
This sounds so cheesy. I can't believe I am doing this.
Summertime in the snow, but I think it is called for because
it has been a balmy three degrees. No negatives in sight.
What else could I expect dating a girl named Sunny?

Bestie to Me

4:30 p.m.

Awwwwwe. You're so cute together.
The way she grabs your hand,
clings to your arm. So cute!
You even match! Well. Kind of.
Her blue eyes. Your blue jeans.
The stars on her shirt. The stars
in your eyes. Wow. She enters
a room and your face… glows.
Lights up. I don't know. But I
feel the gravity in it. How you
orbit each other.

BeaverTails

My hands were so gooey I couldn't fathom
letting go of this treat to hold hers. Thank God
for maple syrup and fried dough and the
sugar stuck to her face that makes the
mess on my face not so obvious. Thank God
she snorts when she laughs and
doesn't use a napkin and chews her nails
and doesn't notice that I chew with my
mouth open and talk too fast when I
don't know what to say and flinch when
she puts her hand on my shoulder and still
stutter though we've been dating for a month.

Do not start an undergraduate degree unless prepared to spend thousands of dollars on coffee. Sudden acquisition of a girlfriend, boyfriend, date mate, or situationship will result in exponentially more spending on silly little treats when combined with a university degree. Your student loans are not designed to be spent on your romantic partner's Venti Iced Caramel Macchiato with almond milk, light ice, and a pump of chocolate syrup. Dating as a post-secondary student may result in being broke.

I'm not… great at this dating thing.
I like… working. I don't know.
Going to uni. Stacking shelves.
Stopping at Tims to get my free donut
at my new favourite location.

I'm not… an outdoors kind of girl, guy, whatever.
I like… this January cold. Blanketed indoors.
Coffee dates wrapped in caramel syrup.
Study dates where I hear about her art classes
and practice identifying bird anatomy.

I'm not… loud with my pride. But
I like… the heat in my cheeks when
she grabs my hand in public, and how
our fingers look linked in the light
of the clear winter sun.

Before I cut my hair, I had the most
elaborate looks. Twisted braids wrapped
into a bun. Flat iron curls that
defied gravity. I went chop chop.
I went to a Clearance Clips and got a
short pixie-fade-undercut thing
nearly a year ago. In my mirror,
I see a girl I don't recognize. In my hands,
I twirl a new girl's gold into loose braids.

"Wow! This is beautiful. When did you learn to do this?"
I shrug and smile, watching my hands mimic my mother's.
"A while ago. I'm glad you like it."

Sonnet (In Spirit, Not in Format)

I'm a yearner, as you've learned.
I haven't earned the words to say so.
I think you need more heartbreak
for that, but I just need her eyes. Oh.
That was horrible. Shakespeare would
roll his eyes. But I never said I was a
writer, just that I was hers. I'm a future
penguin-ologist, not a poet. I'm just a
girl. I'm just a girl. Well… not technically,
but that's another kind of yearning for
late nights. This is for daylight and the
glint in her eye when she says hi.

HAVE IT ALL

My work has only begun,
and yet there is already a
wrinkle. A twist. A girl.
But can't I build a career
and make a little time for
a coffee date? Let's be
honest, I talk to the fish toys,
not girls. Customers like me
when I do my job, but I
don't know how to do this.
She keeps saying yes to coffee dates
and yay! But, what now?

I Paid My Student Fees Today

My free trial done.

My subscription begun.

I hope it's money well spent.

The green glow of the software logo looms over me. With shaking hands, I press "Enable Editing," fully expecting a thousand rows of white to pierce my eyes in the dark of the university library. My gaze is lost in the countless menu options. If I choose bar graph, am I doomed to misrepresent my lab data? If I use VLOOKUP, am I really asking for XLOOKUP? 10% of my grade sinks into the pit of my stomach.

When I use Excel or coding software
and it stops working, I get this red
serif font error message, then this
horrendous zero in my gradebook.
I go to my professor's office hours and
receive a "You just need to keep trying.
Practice makes perfect" platitude
from Professor Loves-Math.
That should have been her name,
but instead she lives with the irony
of her real name: Professor English.

A third-year statistic course should
teach me how to conduct significant
proper penguin research, but not
when my teacher doesn't teach.

THE G.O.A.T. [1]

A queer girl's, guy's, whatever's
favourite prof is rarely the balding white guy.
But hear me out: an instructor who instructs
with office hours where he is in the office
ready to answer questions with answers
not generalized, not a riddle, not useless.

My opinions of him may be high because
my grades are so, or because he said he will go
write me a recommendation letter for the
famed summer fish gut internship.
But how could I not appreciate a pro?

So I scroll over Excel and will pay attention,
nod along, make the constant eye contact
of the favourite student, and do well in this class
(maybe… probably… hopefully).

1. Slang for the "greatest of all time"

GIRL, GUY, WHATEVER

Mid-conversation, mid-lab, mid-observation of
bird skulls, cranial kinesis, and temporal fenestrae (look it up),
my lab partner stops and asks:
"Oh yeah. What are your pronouns again?"

Uh- why should I know?

Mirror, Mirror

A mirror should not be hung next to the shower.
It is awkward. It is humiliating. I run
into the shower to avoid Victoria's secret
that I know I have no reason to hide.

I thought I wore baggy clothes for comfort.
I spend all day in libraries and working anyways,
but maybe my sweaters are worn to cloak
a body tattooed with insecurity.

But as she takes me to drag shows, art exhibits, gay bars,
and I see men who created themselves, pictures of
bodies like mine that don't have to hide, I see a reflection
of a body that is not mine, but could be with a new label.

BOY, LET ME TELL YOU SOMETHING

I don't just dream of her.
Sometimes I fantasize
cutting my hair, switching
schools, cutting my skirts,
switching my look. I lay in
bed and imagine names.
Boy, I dream of being you.
And boy is it annoying.
There is enough on my mind.
There is enough to dream
about without a boy
haunting my sleep.

Drawn Out

I only draw penguins. Black and white
blobs that I can scribble with sharpies,
ignoring composition and light. Now
Sunny, she can draw penguins with
their feathers swirled in stars, beaks
as detailed as a certain Italian chapel
that I can never remember the name of.

What an honour it was when she decided
to draw me. The tangy smell of graphite,
pencils, and paper fills my nose as I sit
so so still. Every muscle is tensed from
my perch on the edge of the library chair.

What an honour it was when she left
the page in my book for me to find, for me
to see short hair with a greyed trans flag pin.
Five stripes in alternating shades drawn with
the care of someone willing to sit and stare
and see who you really are.

SELF-PORTRAIT

She paints my portrait better than
I ever could. Fingers draw on my
clay-mask. Sliced cucumbers on my eyes,
trusting her to paint someone with
perfect skin and a symmetrical nose and…
A cold sinks in as the mask hardens and
her fingers disappear. "Sunny?" "I'm here."
The warmth returns. Her paintbrushes run
through my hair, careful not to smudge the art.

How Dare the Academically Challenging Degree Academically Challenge Me

My girlfriend. No. The girl I have
gone on dates with cradles my
child. My baby. The flashcards
I spent nine months developing.
She tests me. She babbles
scientific words. She sounds out
Latin names of fish, herps, birds, and
mammals. She claps her hands
when I am right. I cry when I fail
to spell *Oncorhynchus mykiss* for
the ninth time. Then we laugh
at photos of puffer fish.

Dating is dating.
Who cares about the words? I
certainly… don't care.

Gay and ignoring the deepening gayness of our relationship,
I see my queerness in more ways. The days
Professor English accidentally called me "he"
were the days after my friend helped me
shave my head. I kind of liked how his mistake
made my head fizzy, buzzed.
It itched something in my brain.

The day my boss accidentally
called me "they" was the day before
Sunny dyed my hair purple because
she mis-mixed the dye. She pretends
she is not colour blind and I kind of enjoy
how these mistakes keep happening.

Not queer as in strange. Not queer as in
fuck you. But queer as in very gay. As in
pointing at the rainbow cake at Sobeys
and saying "me." As in Doc Martins and
high-waisted jeans. As in thumbs up and
finger guns bi because I can't choose one.
As in flirting with all my friends, and we're
all kidding but completely serious because
if you're down, I'm down. Because I love you
and I don't know what that means and I
don't know how to tell you, but I know I will
hold your hand every time we go to a concert.

MY GIRL, BILL

What if I chose the name Bill?
I could go by anything really.
It's not that hard to change my
name tag at work. Or I could
be Bob. Or Maurice. Maybe not those.
I'm not sure. I kind of like my
name. Bill is a bit of a leap.
And a little silly. Do I seem like
a Bill to you? Buried in a library
with my colourful flag on my bag?
But how funny would it be for
someone to sing "my girl, Bill?" to me.

HOUSEHOLD NAME

"You're too young to go as Bill,"
my mom tells me when I say
"I'm not a girl. I don't want to go by
[REDACTED] anymore."

A pressure builds in my chest
as I watch her ponder my choices.

"I'm going to call you Billy."

A tornado erupts from my breath of relief.
My head spins as the household name that
fell on me is lifted from my shoulders.

An Answer for My Lab Partner

When I was asked what I wanted to be when I grew up,
I answered: Penguin Doctor. No question. No hesitation.
When I learnt that the aquarium was hiring with
potential for growth,
I applied the moment the job was listed on Indeed.
When I met Sunny and she asked me if I collected Tims points,
I fell hard and fast as soon as our eyes met.

I am not going to wait to think about the name "Bill,"
about using he/him. This isn't a whim. This is a choice.
Right here. Right now. I am telling Professor G.O.A.T.
to put Bill on his endorsement letter today, after lab,
after I tell Dad.

SCARY AS A CAR CRASH

I came out with the sunrise.
It was February… so, cold as shit on the prairies.
And I was catching a ride early as Dad went to work.

Snow blew across the highway.
Almost there and the car had finally defrosted.
I could wiggle my toes again. My fingers tingled,
red because I didn't wear gloves when I brushed
the snow off 20 minutes ago as a gesture of good will
to chip away the ice from my father's
"It's too early for this" scowl.

My cheeks burned, but they were rosy because of
more than the chill.
It was the thrill (or the fear induced cold sweat) of telling him.
The sun blinds me from just beneath the visor. My frosty
breath reveals relief that I won't see his reaction.

He pays the most attention if you sit next to him.
No eye contact, facing forward on an ice-ridden highway.
Alone, half asleep, I thought there would be no better time to
tell this red-neck plumber that his kid is not only queer, but
trans too.

He kind of answered me. He scratched his beard and asked
if I was coming home for dinner that weekend.

Coming Out as Trans Reminded Me

I read that being gay, and wanting to live loud,
means that before you sit your mother down,
you need to plan for the off chance that
your family does not love you unconditionally.

And that's why being gay fucks you up.

There is no Godly fire to ruin you, besides the
burn of that first spark. There is only the taste of
char in your mouth as you choke on the words

"Mom, I'm bi. I like girls and guys."

And then the smoke fills your lungs as you
wait that moment, that beat, for her to hear
you through the crackle of your racing heart.
And she loves you so so much. But what if?

It Had to Go Wrong at Some Point

"It's just too much work for me to use your new name. You'll always be [REDACTED]."

Professor, I understand, but my name is-

"It's just a phase. You're too young to know."

I would really appreciate it if-

"No."

BUT THE DOGGOS LOVE ME

When every puppy I pass asks for pets
and gives me kisses and wiggles, and when
the geese sit next to me on the hill where
we chill because they have no goslings,
I am not attacked or bitten or honked at.
The wind does not nip at my nose and
the sun glows on our feathers.

I know the buildings whisper about our graffiti
and our ripped clothes and the holes in our ears,
but I can hear the purring of your cat on my lap.

The concrete might find us too rough,
but I cannot be "against nature" when
my nature is pet-friendly.

I am only asking for three simple words.
Boy. He. Him. Another third of the class
hears this every day. A hundred students.
Why can't there be one more?

Did you know that at Tim Hortons,
you can ask for vanilla Iced Capps,
chocolate Iced Capps, and even Oreo Iced Capps.
I just ask for a plain one. No syrups.
No neopronouns. No sprinkles.
I didn't even ask him to correct others.

The lovely Tims workers get it right.
My favourite Tims worker gets it right.
Why can't he?

If Only I Were Mid-Nap, Not Mid-Semester

What am I doing in Professor English's stats course?
I am just here to learn how to learn about penguins.
To learn how to look at data and see new information,
fun facts to pull out of my back pocket for when I
have a real job at an aquarium, or teach, or do research.
I do not need to memorize stupid-ass equations I could make
a computer run or simply never use again. I should drop
this class. I should drop Professor G.O.A.T.'s [2] class.
I should drop out. This used to be about the excitement of
simply seeing or holding a penguin one day, caring for a
flightless feathered one. But one day can never be today if I
fail these stupid-ass courses. I should just leave the research
to the institution and glance at the birds as I walk to the gift
shop.

2. New slang for "get out, abominable turd"

Sunny Days Convince Me Not to Quit

"Take a breath

unclench those fists.

Wash your hair in the clouds.

Release the steam from your ears.

Hear it whistle

then let it fade.

My love,

you are here.

I am here.

Your wingèd friends are here.

Don't worry yourself

over scraped knees and loud voices

when you have

the stars.

Let your steam fade.

You are not an engine."

JUST PRETEND

"It's not a big deal."

I worship my silly little lattes.
They do not drop. I do not spill.
But those words tumble my cup
and drain my coffee onto
my pants, my shoes, my socks.
My jaw drops to the floor.

She sputters, stutters to help
clean up my mess, clean up her words.

"I mean it's just one class,
one professor, one semester.
You can just ignore it. Right, babe?"

Five things I see. Four things I hear. Or is it four things I smell?
No. Three things I smell. Two things I feel. One thing I taste.
White board. Half desk. Notepad. Pen. Highlighter.
Professor G.O.A.T. talking. Student coughing.
Fluorescent lights buzzing.
Phone dinging. Metallic iPads. Students who need more
deodorant or perfume. Students who need
less deodorant or perfume.
Fluffy sweater. Hard chair back. Mint gum.

A zoology course is not my end. It does not decide whether
my friends love me, or if I have work tonight, or if Sunny
will pick me up after my shift to see the new romcom.
 If I sit still in the back, pretend I am still her,
put the wrong name on my test, he will never notice.
I will pass. I will get the job.

Let's Take a Break from this Gay Shit

My midterm is tomorrow, and dammit-
my supervisor shouldn't have let me
bring my books and papers to work.
How dare I be allowed to do flashcards
between check-outs instead of being
checked-out? Where is my stack of
orca stuffies to pillow my heavy head
for an hour or four or eight before I
have to face my chewed HB pencils
without a polar bear on the end to
remind me it's okay if I fail this one?
There will always be work tomorrow.

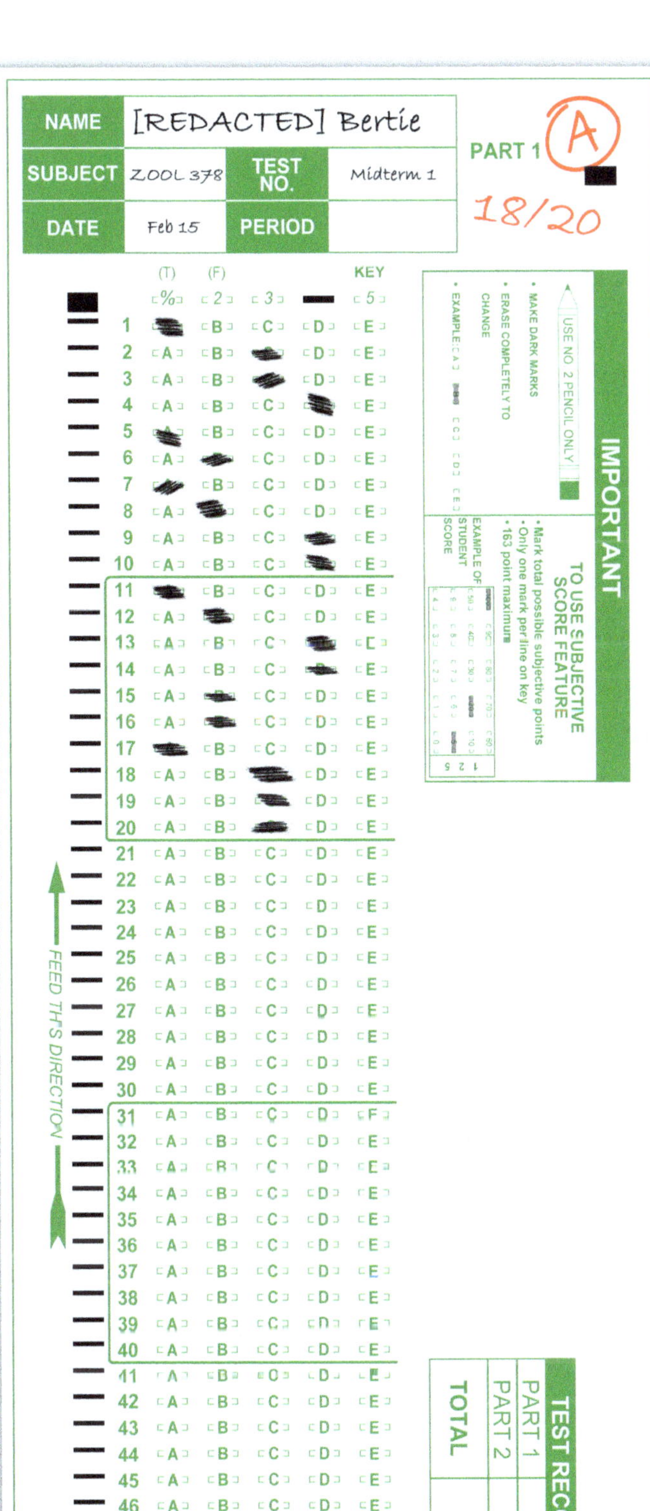

NAME [REDACTED] Bertie
SUBJECT ZOOL 378
TEST NO. Midterm 1
DATE Feb 15
PERIOD
PART 1
A
18/20
(T) (F) KEY
USE NO 2 PENCIL ONLY
IMPORTANT
TO USE SUBJECTIVE SCORE FEATURE
MAKE DARK MARKS
ERASE COMPLETELY TO CHANGE
EXAMPLE
Mark total possible subjective points
Only one mark per line on Key
163 point maximum
EXAMPLE OF STUDENT SCORE
FEED THIS DIRECTION
TEST RECORD
PART 1
PART 2
TOTAL

Like an Itchy Sweater

"Yes, [REDACTED]. You're correct, miss."

"Here's how you can do better in your next lab, miss."

"No, [REDACTED], but you're close."

Paper cuts are knicks, mini-injuries
that could be avoided
if I was more careful.
if I wore gloves.
if I stopped using paper.

But gloves are itchy,
and I handwrite all of my notes.

So I will ignore the way the
soap stings when I wash
my hands after my lab.

Seven Points for Rooster

This day has felt like seven.
This morning was last week.
I feel that grimy layer from
too much sugar and too many
days since I brushed my teeth.
I should have put my phone down
last night, this morning, 1 a.m.
But we were texting. How could
I pass up this chance when she
can't sleep and I can't sleep, so
we can play Scrabble from
opposite sides of town?

I'm Not Pouting

"It's not a big deal."
Mom's right. It's not. Really.

"Just ignore him."
Sunny's right. It will be fine.

I will be fine. I will be fine. I will be fine.
I will be fine. I will be fine. I will be fine.

"Hey, bestie. Are you sure? We can fight this
if you want. I'll help you."

"Nah." I dismiss. I evade.
It's best not to think about how this man
has my future in his hands and
what would happen if I fought this.

I have done the thing.
The midterm is wrote. Written.
No matter. It is done, and
I can now study penguins.
Not fish. Not frogs. Not caecilians,
whatever those are. 5 p.m. can
be for David Attenborough,
not practice exams. Kids have
fluffy penguins on their beds.
Is it weird that I do too?
Are my dreams not realistic
enough for working hours?

CHOCOLATE MILK

After I passed my midterm, my mum and dad
took me to get chocolate milkshakes. Then
the next morning, I had chocolate milk in
my cornflakes and chocolate chips in my
pancakes. Then Sunny surprised me with
chocolate ice cream cones after lunch,
then she met my family, and I had more
chocolate milk with my dinner because
why not? And then I had leftover chocolate
chip pancakes as a midnight snack. And then
I had a banana because I would have fallen
into a sugar coma if my weekend got any sweeter.

MORE LIKE A STORY, BUT FELT LIKE A POEM

So yeah. She met the parents.
But it wasn't so bad because
it wasn't to
"meet the parents."

It was to celebrate that I
did fine on a midterm.
So she never really
"met the parents."

Neither have I, really.
Not hers anyways.
Another's? Yes. Kind of.
His. "His" to me. "Hers" to his parents,
So "hers" to me when I was at his house.
He wasn't out yet (obviously), so I never
"met the parents."

I was his… friend?
And while I was out,
and his parents glared at me in public,
his mom laughed at my jokes and
his dad served me ribs.
That was the best meal I ever tasted,
but that meal with Sunny was better than any barbecue
because her hand melted into mine when she said

"It is nice to meet you Mr. and Mrs. Future Penguin-ologist's
Parents."

Then Sunny and I spent $50 each making shitty pottery
and we brought friends and she painted little pink flowers
and then I dropped my bowl and we moulded it back into a
wonky pot that leaves us cackling because it looks a lot
like my best friend's head with a really long forehead.

Then we all had a *Death Becomes Her* watch party
and I made pizza for a vegetarian, a pepperoni nut,
and a friend allergic to tomatoes, and while I was ready
to drop it in the oven, let it burn, and make them cook
for themselves, they loved it and I want to do that again.

Then bestie showed up with more chocolate ice cream
and a trans flag they got at a queer book club at the library,
and for a moment, this is enough. This is fine.

Round and Round

after Fuck You *sang by* Lily Allen

"Fuck you" bounces in my earbud,
the one I haven't lost yet. Lord knows
what happened to the left one. My foot
taps as that right beat bops with the
speed bumps on the bus. Then as if the song
were a summons for the beasts at my church,
a woman with her domed, towering pixie and
those angled bangs across her forehead
starts pursing her lips at the two sweethearts
holding hands across from her. I can read
the comment on the tip of her tongue
and all I can think is "fuck you."

After I finish this last assignment,

I promise I will remove email

from my phone and remember to

text her back before I go to work.

After I finish this last shift,

I promise we can go for that walk.

Movie. Bowling. Star gazing at the

observatory. I have student access. We can go.

After I finish this last project, exam, lab.

After I finish this busy day at the gift shop during

the last kindergarten field trip to the aquarium of the year…

She will have to work, so I will pick up another shift.

Up at 3 a.m.

There's a rhythm in the 30 minutes
after head hits pillow but before eyes
listen. It's when my mind takes the
drumsticks, bangs on the cymbals,
scratches at the electric guitar. When
I close my eyes, I see her. She can
open my mind, make me fly with fairy dust
or leave shadows in my window. It really
depends if I was whimsical enough
that day. Did I bring that pink drink
to work? Or did I forget to kiss the back
of her hand when she wished me goodbye?

MY BARCODE MISCODED

There's a point half-way through a shift,
where I realize I have scanned the same
fluffy penguin pom-pom keychain so many times
that the inventory must be endless.

I could dive into a pile of fluff and never
reach the bottom. Drown in button eyes and
choke on lengths of looped chains, swimming
to a promotion as realistic as gaining my prof's respect.

Beep. Beep. Beep. Goes the scanner. It
resounds as my mind wanders to the
Beep. Beep. Beep. Of a droning man reading my name,
attaching the wrong tag… again.

Why am I showing up to a class
that is taking me nowhere? Not nowhere.
Here. Where the Beep. Beep. Beep. Of a
deadname tells me to woman the fuck up.

Your Thoughts and Prayers

I was stacking copies of Marcus Pfister's
The Rainbow Fish, grinning at how the
rainbow scales matched my suspenders,
when an older woman with dyed blonde roots
stopped me, grabbed my hands, and told me
"You're so brave." She announced this
after a certain Premier made another statement
about trans youth, and another cross walk
was stripped of life. She gave me
that concerned, hopeful smile that
makes my toes curl. All I could do was
smile back and wish her a good day.

Bestie Was Right

My wound's infected.
I should have listened, cleaned it. Am
I too late to heal?

The third largest seal in the world,

with few natural predators,

has many options for prey.

They have those sharp, one-inch teeth.

But do not need to use them.

Why work for your meal when you can drift,

and filter a swarm of krill?

When they must, of course, these predators

eat seals or penguins and I can't guilt someone for eating.

For living. Even if it means killing penguins.

And like orcas and small human children, leopard seals

play with their food, toss them into the air for

a penguin's first and last chance at flight.

They chase, let them think they got away, then chomp!

I don't know if I'm getting away or if

there are teeth at my feet. I'm running

from this man, monster, whatever. I can feel it in the

race of my heart and the weight on my chest

and how I'm glancing over my shoulder, waiting

for him to fail me out of his course or refuse to be
my reference because

I'm the student he wants me to be, but not the gender.

And he smiles and waves, and shows off those sharp teeth
when I don't correct him. But I can't keep swimming away
when I know my heart will give out like this.

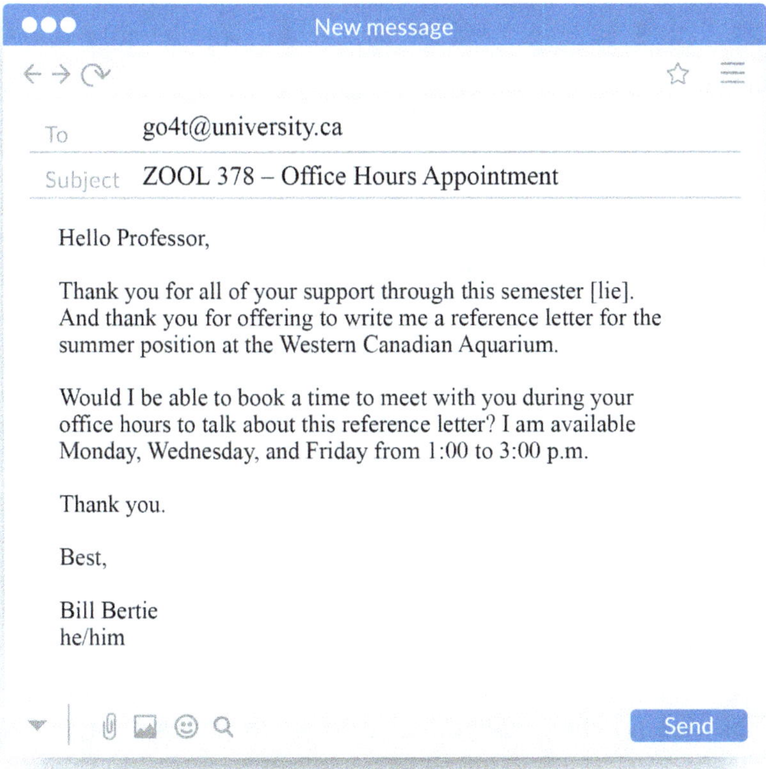
New message

To   go4t@university.ca

Subject   ZOOL 378 – Office Hours Appointment

Hello Professor,

Thank you for all of your support through this semester [lie].
And thank you for offering to write me a reference letter for the
summer position at the Western Canadian Aquarium.

Would I be able to book a time to meet with you during your
office hours to talk about this reference letter? I am available
Monday, Wednesday, and Friday from 1:00 to 3:00 p.m.

Thank you.

Best,

Bill Bertie
he/him

Send

After that well-crafted, masterpiece of an email,
how could this meeting have gone so wrong?

Polite. Sincere. In my best-pressed shirt.
Confident. Calm. With proper posture too.

Yet still he sneered when I asked to be called Bill.
I saw the yellow of his teeth, smelt the bitterness
of his coffee breath. He dismissed. He argued
like I asked him to change my grade from an F to an A.

Polite. Sincere. I used civil language.
Confident. Calm. I was courteous.

"I understand you may not agree, but…"

"This doesn't change anything about me as your student,
but…"

"I hear you, but…"

No. He said no. Then asked, more like told, me to leave.
He had an "appointment" to run to.
Then I got an email about him revoking the reference.

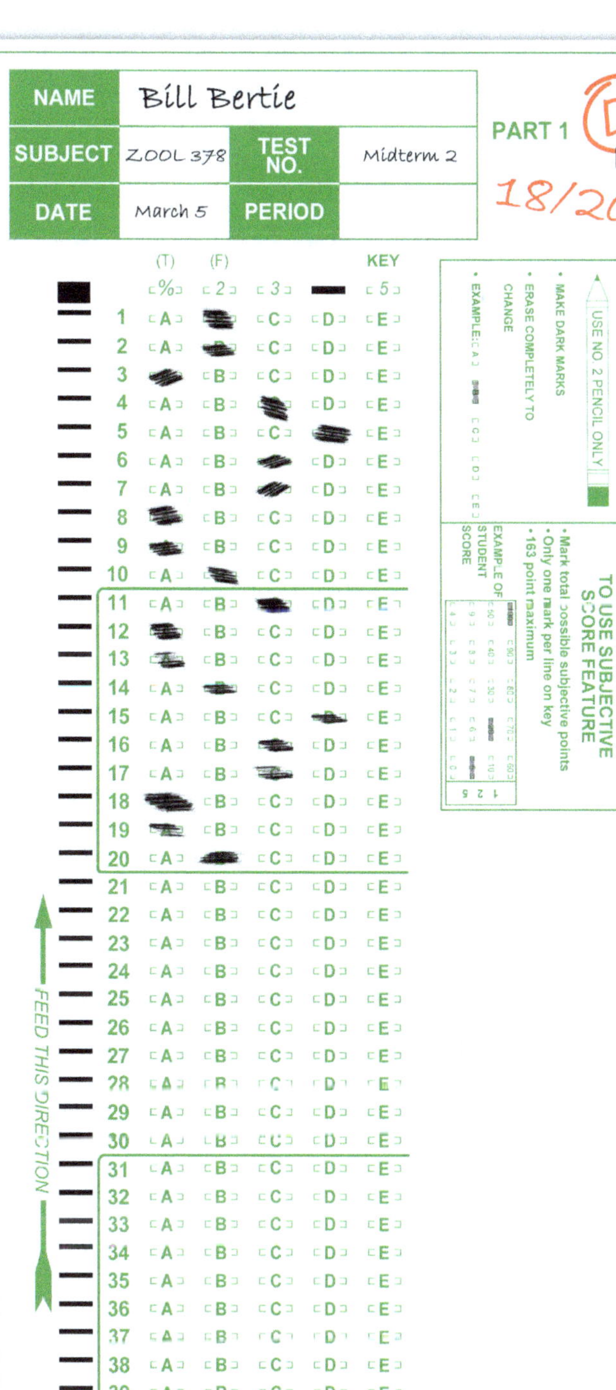

NAME   Bill Bertie
SUBJECT   ZOOL 378   TEST NO.   Midterm 2
DATE   March 5   PERIOD
PART 1   D-
18/20
(T)   (F)   KEY
IMPORTANT
USE NO. 2 PENCIL ONLY
MAKE DARK MARKS
ERASE COMPLETELY TO CHANGE
EXAMPLE: A
TO USE SUBJECTIVE SCORE FEATURE
Mark total possible subjective points
Only one mark per line on key
163 point maximum
EXAMPLE OF STUDENT SCORE
FEED THIS DIRECTION
TEST
PART
PART
TOTAL

Why Is the Winter Semester Always Harder?

In my second semester, first winter semester,
I failed chemistry. I failed chemistry so bad that
I am surprised that university administration
let me retake it in the spring semester.

In my fourth semester, second winter semester,
I didn't fail, but I almost lost my job because
I was pulling all-nighters and falling asleep
during my lunch break. I was late… a lot.

At least life is consistent. I slipped on the ice,
fell on my ass twice on my way home from work tonight.

I stepped through my apartment door and
I dropped my bag. I didn't put it back under my desk.
I kicked off my shoes and left them in front of the door.
I plopped down onto the couch, and I didn't move.

I Made Myself Soup

I sat in the tub
with flowers and candles, and
simmered until cooked.

I Called My Mom

I sobbed. I wiped snot
across my pjs. I made
no sense. She listened.

I Ate Nachos with Bestie

Gooey food to eat
out our feelings, until we
can fight together.

SINTERING

When snowflakes land, they reach
other flurries and form bonds.
Not hydrogen bonds, but their own
coagulation of sorts.

Leanne Betasamosake Simpson [3]
related this process to how humans
interact with each other. Chatting. Babbling.
Bonding over our connection as people.

I read her book and imagined cheesy cartoon snowflakes
holding hands, singing a Whoville carol
as they discover the joy of friendship.

Then I push my friend into the snow and
we laugh when they pull me down with them.
The snow melts into my jeans, my dollar store gloves.

Then the cold slides down the back of my coat,
but I don't shiver.

3. Leanne Betasamosake Simpson. *Theory of Water: Nishnaabe Maps to the Times Ahead.* Knopf Canada by Haymarket Books, 2025.

I CAN FIGHT THIS

ing it. I'm doing it. I'm doing it. I'm doing it. I'm doing it. I'm doing it. I'm doi
doing it. I'm doing it. I'm doing it. I'm doing it. I'm doing it. I'm doing it. I'm
it. I'm doing it. I'm doing it. I'm doing it. I'm doing it. I'm doing it. I'm doing i
ing it. I'm doing it. I'm doing it. I'm doing it. I'm doing it. I'm doing it. I'm doi
doing it. I'm doing it. I'm doing it. I'm doing it. I'm doing it. I'm doing it. I'm
it. I'm doing it. I'm doing it. I'm doing it. I'm doing it. I'm doing it. I'm doing i
ing it. I'm doing it. I'm doing it. I'm doing it. I'm doing it. I'm doing it. I'm doi
doing it. I'm doing it. I'm doing it. I'm doing it. I'm doing it. I'm doing it. I'm
it. I'm doing it. I'm doing it. I'm doing it. I'm doing it. I'm doing it. I'm doing i
ing it. I'm doing it. I'm doing it. I'm doing it. I'm doing it. I'm doing it. I'm doi
doing it. I'm doing it. I'm doing it. I'm doing it. I'm doing it. I'm doing it. I'm
it. I'm doing it. I'm doing it. I'm doing it. I'm doing it. I'm doing it. I'm doing i
ing it. I'm doing it. I'm doing it. I'm doing it. I'm doing it. I'm doing it. I'm doi
doing it. I'm doing it. I'm doing it. I'm doing it. I'm doing it. I'm doing it. I'm
it. I'm doing it. I'm doing it. I'm doing it. I'm doing it. I'm doing it. I'm doing i
ing it. I'm doing it. I'm doing it. I'm doing it. I'm doing it. I'm doing it. I'm doi
doing it. I'm doing it. I'm doing it. I'm doing it. I'm doing it. I'm doing it. I'm
it. I'm doing it. I'm doing it. I'm doing it. I'm doing it. I'm doing it. I'm doing i
ing it. I'm doing it. I'm doing it. I'm doing it. I'm doing it. I'm doing it. I'm doi
doing it. I'm doing it. I'm doing it. I'm doing it. I'm doing it. I'm doing it. I'm
it. I'm doing it. I'm doing it. I'm doing it. I'm doing it. I'm doing it. I'm doing i
ing it. I'm doing it. I'm doing it. I'm doing it. I'm doing it. I'm doing it. I'm doi
doing it. I'm doing it. I'm doing it. I'm doing it. I'm doing it. I'm doing it. I'm
it. I'm doing it. I'm doing it. I'm doing it. I'm doing it. I'm doing it. I'm doing i
ing it. I'm doing it. I'm doing it. I'm doing it. I'm doing it. I'm doing it. I'm doi
doing it. I'm doing it. I'm doing it. I'm doing it. I'm doing it. I'm doing it. I'm
it. I'm doing it. I'm doing it. I'm doing it. I'm doing it. I'm doing it. I'm doing i
ing it. I'm doing it. I'm doing it. I'm doing it. I'm doing it. I'm doing it. I'm doi
doing it. I'm doing it. I'm doing it. I'm doing it. I'm doing it. I'm doing it. I'm
it. I'm doing it. I'm doing it. I'm doing it. I'm doing it. I'm doing it. I'm doing i
ing it. I'm doing it. I'm doing it. I'm doing it. I'm doing it. I'm doing it. I'm do

SPOOKY SHIT IN THE SHADOWS

"Sunny, I have to deal with this.
There is no way he is allowed to give me a D-
for the same grade I received an A for a month ago.
This isn't fair. I can't be happy and not be me."

I've never felt a chill so cold, a shiver so far down my back
as when I told the embodiment of sunshine, brighter than
the prairie sky,
that I couldn't sit in the dark for a moment longer.

I support you. You

know that. But this is a lot.

It's just one guy, babe.

"Hey, honey?" "Yeah?" "I think we should
just be friends." "Oh?" "Yeah. Wait- no. Don't
drop my hand." "But you said we should just
be friends." "Yeah, but like gay friends. Friends
that are actually close. And intimate. And
friendly. Friends that care, but-" "But don't kiss."
"Yeah." "Oh." "Oh? Is that a problem?" "No! Well,
yeah. Not in a creepy I'm only in it for the kisses
way, but in a I love what we have way." "But is
what we have really a relationship? You treat me
like you treat your best friend." "You are my
best friend." "But shouldn't I be more?"

THIRD ACT BREAK UP

It's one of those tales, you see.
Maybe she bleeds out in my arms
or maybe she just leaves. But
either way, our story doesn't end
with an epilogue where five years
later we have kids and a house.

We had that perfect foot-poppin' kiss,
and we fought back-to-back with
our swords raised, ready to go down
in a blaze of glory for the other.

But as we both grew up wearing corsets and dresses,
we end like Hans Christian Andersen.

If you could tell by my shitty metaphors
and repetition, I still don't know
what I'm talking about here. It's
my first love story, so I obviously
haven't learnt how to write them.
And I'm doing well. See. Look how
successful I am. Ignoring that one
horrible zoology class, look at my grades,
my job, my accomplishments for
my age. I have no real experience.
There will be other girls, other jobs.
It doesn't really matter.
There are other books to read.

CRINKLY STOMACHS

The girl working in the Tim Hortons
made my stomach crinkle. It wasn't
the coffee swirling in my bowel, but
the pitter patter of a girl dipped in espresso.

Now there is a wrinkle in the paper.
I can never keep the edges straight.
She stained rings in the pages of my work.

I thought the rain could keep us inside
and she could smile and rave about her sister's cat
until her tongue ran dry, and I could buy
her another coffee. Whatever she wants.
But who knew 24/7 had a last call?

Okay, Maybe I Got Sad

Did you know Willow and Tara were
the first wuh-luh-wuh kiss on television?
I've been rewatching *Buffy the Vampire Slayer,*
and I'm on season 5, buzzing with anticipation.
But I know Tara's just going to die.
Two seasons later she'll get shot, and
nothing will be the same. Because it's
just another show where the gay girl
dies. I want a wedding. Giles could
officiate. Anya could make a funny
speech. But that will never happen.
Why watch the coming seasons,
even if there is a musical episode?

Penguins don't write sad poems
when they shiver in the wind,
so I can turn off the tv and go
back to work, report that douchebag,
then write that next exam with a fair opportunity,
then do that great job feeding flightless birds chum.

I Think

I think I want to study penguins
because I want to live like one.
To be in the blistering cold,
huddled with those I love. It is
dark for six months straight, yet
when the night ends, they
shake off the snow and slide
into the water, and swim after
a fish like they didn't almost
lose a toe. Six months of balmy
zero-degree weather must be
worth their frozen feathers.

MARCH ON

When you're not in university, March is nowhere near
the end of the year. But it is a step away from semester's end,
from starting a summer job I have no guarantee of for now.
Everyone else in the sciences arrives to summer employment
in January. So unless I want to work in a gift shop for
another year, I need to march into student services and demand
help to fix this grade, to fix this discriminatory refusal.
There has to be something in the university bylaws against
transphobia, against whatever just happened back there.

This isn't a war. I'm not trying to start a thing here,
but I am a little pissed because this is taking so long,
and grade disputes are rarely accepted from students.

I never watch three-quels because they are never good. My third trip to office hours this semester couldn't have been in my other courses. There's no drama or struggle, or crushing urge to quit Developmental Biology, or Behavioural Ecology, or Cell Biology, which sound like Scary Movie I, II, and III. Instead, I face the next Hannibal, the Professor English who probably summoned me to eat me alive for missing the deadline for the last… three assignments. She doesn't look like Anthony Hopkins, but her blue eyes are just as eerie from behind her desk, although a little soft, crinkled and… kind.

"Hello, Mr. Bertie. Thank you for meeting with me. Take a seat. I wanted to talk to you about how your semester is going."

"There have been a few
rumours floating down my way.
Do you need to talk?"

THE TRANSCRIPT OF MY BREAK DOWN

She asked me if I was okay and I was caught
like a fish on a hook. Her words spilled my guts.
I anchored my allegations with email threads and
midterms, and I saw this ever-smiling, ever-dimpled
professor sneer like she had a bad taste in her mouth.
Warm eyes turn as cold as ice. Apparently,
he speaks over his female coworkers in meetings,
over her since she switched to the biology department.
Professor English has been fishing for a reason
to show him that he is not the be-all and end-all.

He doesn't decide which students swim forward,
and who stops dead in the water.

I take a mouthful of pizza. Chew. Chew. Chew.
"Okay. Here's the thing, bestie. Prof English said that
how grade percentages align with grade letters
is up to the professor.
So 90% does not have to be an A, but a D- is a little extreme."
Bestie scoffs and scarfs down their own slice.

I take a mouthful of pizza. Chew. Chew. Chew.
"It's allowed, but giving one student a D-
and another an A for the same grade…
Now that is grounds for a grade change."
"Oh, wow. That's great! Have you figured out
 how to get the reference letter back too?"
"No. I am still chewing on that."

I did a clopen for the first time
in a while. Closed and then opened.
Locked and unlocked the keychains
and stuffed animals from their cages.
If I could, I would bring my sleeping bag
under the fish tank arch, watch the water,
spend the night reading the penguins
bed time stories. Robert Munsch will hum
how I will love them forever, and
like them for always. And then they'd splash,
clang clang rattle bing bang on their toys all day.

Monday morning, and my professor is
already spouting gibberish about how
a tail is only a tail if it does not have a
body cavity. This is not an 8 a.m. topic.
This is maybe a 3 p.m. topic when I am
equally tired, but ready for a whimsical
anecdote before the end of class, possibly
about eels vs. snakes, both with reduced
or absent tails. But here I am, no coffee
in hand, peeling my eyes open for another
hour before I have to make flashcards
to remember the time that is passing.

I'VE BETRAYED MY NATION

I am a traitor to my country. I
brought a Starbucks to work. I
didn't know what else to do. I wanted
a coffee, but I didn't want to bring in
Tims because then I'll pass her Tims
and it will be like I'm avoiding her if she
sees the red maple leaf in my hand,
which I am, but that is not the point.
I had to. So I took the opportunity to
see my name written by a hand that doesn't question it.
Where else would I have the chance?
So I asked for a medium at Starbucks.

SUNNY

Her name was Sunny. Yes. She was
blonde. And yes. She always lit up my day,
but she was more than that. She was the
sting of a sunburn after a long day chasing
seagulls at the lake, and the warmth of that
nap afterward. She was the tingling of hot
Cheetos. I lick all the artificial red dust off
my fingers when I miss the taste of her. She was
Sunny. She was my first sunburn.
I don't miss the sticky aloe lotion or how it hurt
to move when she left. But I still smile at the
Cheeto bag sitting underneath my desk.

Oh, well. I was dumped.
Time to stand back up because
I said so. Oh, well.

My Dude-Guy-Person-Thing, Bill

Borrowing Dad's jeans means more gender and more pockets.

Idle hands rest in extra material as I watch my TA give lab instructions.

Lying on the tables are taxidermied ducks, corvids, and seabirds.

Like a try-hard, I raise my hand. "Yes, Bill?"

Bound Tight

I have been out of grade school for a
minute now, but I have only today
bought my first binder. 3-ringed.
2-inch. Just joking. Tight stitch.

Tired of classrooms, I scratch that
itch and flatten that chest because
why not be that boy I fought so
hard for. "A phase," my ass.

My language is crass, but damn it-
his self-satisfied rasp I hear from the back
of the class grates and scrapes
like he knows he has won.

Professor English Says to Be Patient

"Hang on. Just a sec.
Give me a minute. Slow down."
But the clock won't. Please.

Professor English Says to Stay Calm

Around the corner from the gift shop is
an exit, a fire exit for when it all goes to Hell.
For when I pull the alarm. Abort. Abort.

Around the corner of the seas, I see
a red wave of red tape ready to wrap me,
tangle me in wait until I burn with my GPA.
Aboard this ship, I watch the water rise as my
captain tells me to sail on. To ignore the rocks.

Swim away. Abort. Abort. Leave this place. Abort. Abort.
My last day of classes is next week. I can practically touch
the flames of exam heat. But I cannot study with a D-
threatening to pull me under. Abort. Abort.

I can bury myself in papers, in work,
and still be found without a shovel.
Bestie found me in my hole, under a box
of stale pizza, in clothes that should have
been washed a week ago, burrowed in
study material and tears. "Oh, bro.
Have you moved since the start of exam break?"
I shake my head. "Oh, bro. Let's go out.
Tonight. Maybe shower first, but then
let's go dancing or get BeaverTails-
No. No. No. Don't cry! I'm sorry.
We don't have to do any of that.
Let's just take a break."

A FEW COLOURS

I started painting. I thought it
was time to do something creative.
It's mostly blobby penguins and
a few diagrams from my notes,
but it's the start of something. I guess.
I show them to the flightless puffins,
and they squawk, probably
waddling around just because.
They mosey, screech hello.
Maybe they recognize
themselves in the water colours.
I'll show them another tomorrow.

The Day I Became an Exhibit for the Kindergarten Aquarium Field Trip

A little girl stared at my hair.
I had to dye it another colour
because we did the last colour
when we were still a "we" and
that obviously had to go. I wasn't
so sure about this pink. A red or
black might have been less
distracting, but that little girl beamed.
"Look Mom! It's Strawberry Shortcake!"
Maybe I shouldn't have worn my
strawberry shirt that day.
At least someone likes it.

Pushing That Rock Up That Hill for Three More Days

I've studied. I remember. I think.
Even if one course is doomed,
I do not move. A pillar. Tall. Stone.
Like the caryatids before me.

I am no goddess of rock and stability.
But I remember the strengths of
the women who threw the first bricks.
I just keep standing, even when the floor
crumbles beneath me. I just hold
up my chin a little while longer.

Because the history of protest is on my side.
Because someone is standing up for me.

No saviour email,

but the exam begins still.

Deep breaths. Do your best.

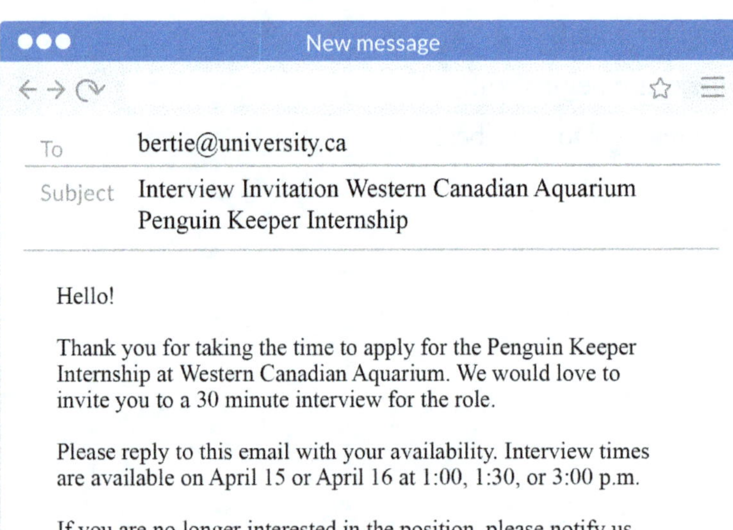
New message
To   bertie@university.ca
Subject   Interview Invitation Western Canadian Aquarium
            Penguin Keeper Internship

Hello!

Thank you for taking the time to apply for the Penguin Keeper
Internship at Western Canadian Aquarium. We would love to
invite you to a 30 minute interview for the role.

Please reply to this email with your availability. Interview times
are available on April 15 or April 16 at 1:00, 1:30, or 3:00 p.m.

If you are no longer interested in the position, please notify us.
We look forward to speaking with you soon.

Best wishes,

- -

Sylvia Johnson, PhD
Western Canadian Aquarium Aquarist
she/her

Bittersweet

Me to Bestie

1:00 a.m.

I got the job

I got the job

I GOT THE JOB

Apparently, the penguin manager vet lady has seen me sitting outside the enclosure everyday and my supervisor at the gift shop put in a good word!

IM SO EXCITED THIS IS SO GOOD OH MY GOD I GOT THE JOB

Prof English also emailed me back and said she couldn't get my grade changed…

BUT I GOT THE JOB!!!

Bestie to Me

1:05 a.m.

Me to Bestie

1:06 a.m.

Happily Ever After
(Fairytale)

Professor G.O.A.T. emailed me with an apology
and Professor English became the new
department head and then made sure he was fired.

I was never deadnamed or misgendered ever again
and I never betrayed my authenticity for
comfort or ease or polite-ness after that day.

Sunny glanced up from behind the counter,
but did not see me at the gift shop,
and wished she had.

Life was easy and I fell in love with a princess new to town,
and saved the day for other students
wanting to fight the cis-stem,
and I became a penguin-ologist (or is it flightless
ornithologist?)

Happily Ever After (Reality)

Fish guts do not smell as pleasant as I imagined.
More like a can of tuna left to cook in a dumpster
than a salted cod baking in cheesy potatoes,
but I am certain these silly little guys smile
back at me at every feeding time.

Professor English assured the penguins and I
were not fed to the leopard seal, so I ended with a B.
"Be patient. He at least respects you as a student."
Be real. He never respected me to begin with.
Be real. I avoid eye contact every time I run into
him in the hallway, and her at work.

Be real. I still eat too much pizza and drink too much coffee.
Be real. Surviving this is proof that even penguins can fly.

Acknowledgements

Thank you first to you, the reader, for taking the time to sit with my poems. Even though the story is fictional, this work is incredibly meaningful to me. Thank you to the Wild Skies Press team, Alexis Marie Chute, Fiona Pearson, and Brooklyn Hollinger. I am so proud of this book, and it would not be possible without you. Thank you for your support, time, and efforts.

Thank you to my broader support network. Thank you to my parents and grandparents for always being there for me. I hope you enjoyed this book and that you do not ask me to read you excerpts (please). Thank you to my friends, especially Keegan Kirchen, Killian Niedzielski, and Sara Morinchuk, who I have been reading and writing with for the longest time. Thank you for proofreading and dealing with my cringey poetry for more than five years now.

Thank you to all the teachers and professors who have supported me not only through writing and learning, but also through experiencing my own internships and growing up. Shout out to Mrs. Boake, my high school English teacher who taught me how amazing poetry can be.

Thank you as well to the broader Edmonton-area writing community including Vers/e Queer Open Mic run by Matthew Stepanic, the writing groups at Strathcona County Library, the Olive Reading Series, and the lovely writers-in-residence who have mentored me, including Nisha Patel and Katie Bickell. Without the continuous mentoring and opportunities to write, this book never would have been written.

TEREN HAZZARD is a transgender writer living on treaty six territory in Amiskwacîwâskahikan (Edmonton, Alberta). His poetry explores the everyday experiences of being queer in Canada. His work can be found in the *Queer Toronto Literary Magazine, Beyond Queer Words,* and *Transit in Motion* Strathcona County bus art. His poem, "Dance with Us, Girly Girl" is the 1st place winner of the 2025 Centre for Literature in Canada Poetry Contest. Teren is currently pursuing a Bachelor of Science in Environmental and Conservation Sciences at the University of Alberta and is excited to integrate what he learns in his courses into his writing.

Other Books by Wild Skies Press

  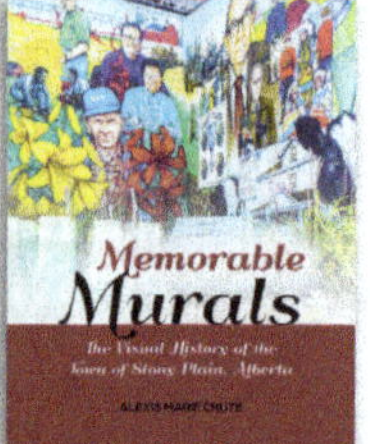

 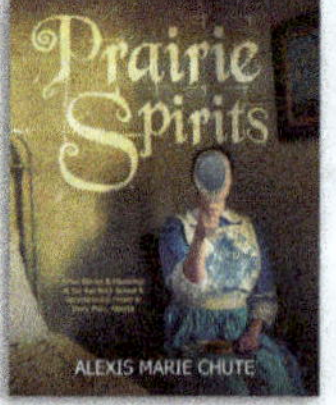 

 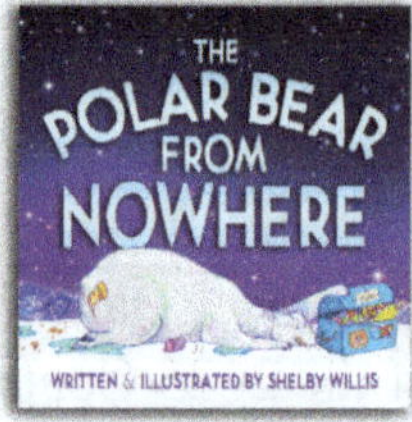  

www.WildSkiesPress.com